this book belongs to

children's choice®

A Children's Choice® Book Club Edition From Scholastic Book Services

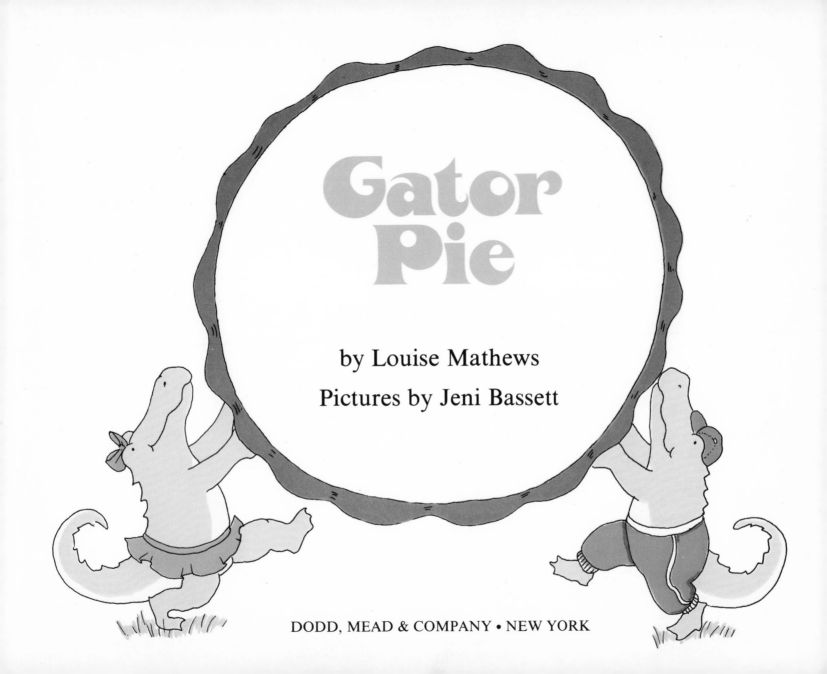

Gator Pie

by Louise Mathews

Pictures by Jeni Bassett

DODD, MEAD & COMPANY • NEW YORK

For Our Families

This is Alvin and this is Alice.

One day they found a pie on a table
near the edge of the swamp.

It was a whole pie that had not been cut.
"I wonder what kind it is," said Alice.
"Let's eat it and find out!" cried Alvin.

"Don't grab," said Alice, slapping his paw.
"I'll cut it first."

"Now, let's see," said Alice.
"There are two of us, so we need two pieces."

"Then cut two halves," said Alvin.
But before she did . . .

An alligator stomped up with
a nasty look in his eye.
"Gimme some pie," he growled.

"Three gators," gulped Alice.
"That means three pieces."

"Cut three one-thirds," muttered Al.
But before she did . . .

A new gator came and slithered onto the bench.
"Eating pie?" he asked, with a terrible grin.
His teeth looked very sharp.

"Y-y-yes," said Alice. "That means—"

"Four pieces," Al grunted.
"Cut four one-fourths."
But before she did . . .

Four gators appeared, swaggering like gangsters.
"Hello, little gators," they said, with a sneer.
"We hear you're giving out pie."

"Oh," murmured Alice.
"I guess we are."
She counted their fat, warty tails.

"Eight gators—eight pieces,"
she said to Al.

"Cut eight one-eighths," he grumbled.
But before she did . . .

Splash, sputter, and crash, a ton of gators
marched out of the swamp like an army.
"We've come to get our pie," they said.
Their wet scales flashed like armor in the sun.

Alice's teeth went clickety-clack in her snout.
"Why, yes, of course," she gasped.
"Pie for everyone!"

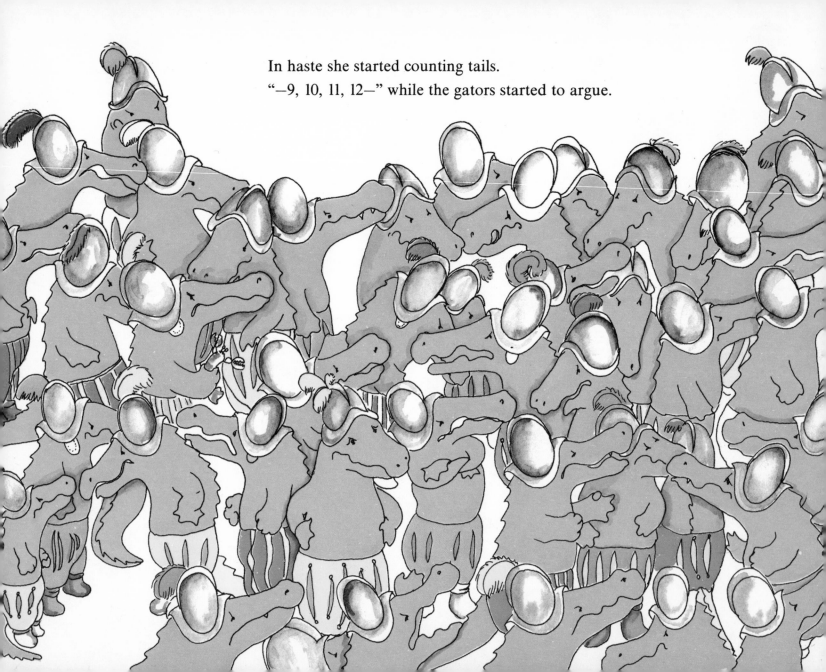

In haste she started counting tails.
"—9, 10, 11, 12—" while the gators started to argue.

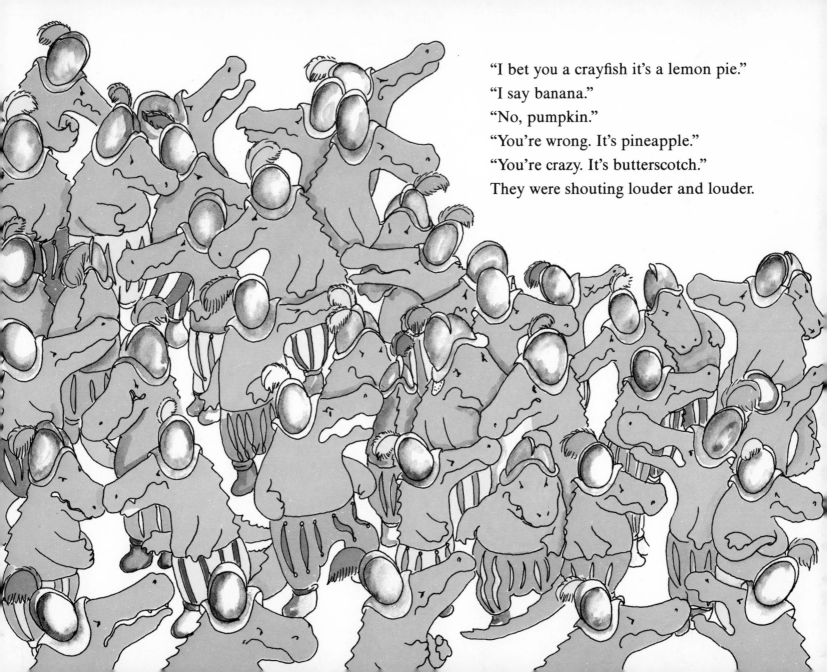

"I bet you a crayfish it's a lemon pie."

"I say banana."

"No, pumpkin."

"You're wrong. It's pineapple."

"You're crazy. It's butterscotch."

They were shouting louder and louder.

"—98, 99, 100," said Alice.
"Oh, my, a hundred pieces,"
she sighed.

"You'll have to cut one hundred one-hundredths,"
Al groaned, trying to think in the noise.

"O-ooh," said Alice, "that will be hard.
"If they think I've cut the pie unfairly
they'll start an awful fight."

It took a long time to cut the pie into
one hundred slices.

Alice did her very best
to make each piece the same size.

"Oh, dear," Alice whispered when she finished, "the pieces are so tiny!"

"Too tiny," said Alvin.

"And what if they're *not* all the same size," Alice groaned.

Suddenly Alvin jumped up on the table.
He pointed to the pie.

"Pick a piece!" he shouted.
"We're not sure they are all the same size."

"Don't say that!" squeaked Alice in a fright.
But Alvin winked at her.

"I'll take this piece," said the smiley gator,
sliding his paw toward the pie.
"No, you won't!" snarled the fattest gator,
biting his tail.

Then the fattest gator reached for a slice.
Somebody pulled him down.
Soon they were kicking, scratching,
snarling, snapping,
chomping and stomping on tails.

Ninety-eight growling gators
were fighting for the biggest slice.

Alvin and Alice held their breaths.
Then Alvin nudged Alice.
"Now!" he cried. "Grab the pie!"

They skittered past the pile of twisting gators
and raced off into the swamp.

1/2

All by themselves they divided up the pie,
piece by piece, fair and square.
They each got fifty slices,
exactly one-half of the pie.

1/8   1/4   1/3   1/100

That was better than one-eighth, or one-fourth,
or even one-third of the pie.
And it was much, much better than one-hundredth,
which is just a tiny sliver.

"How lucky for us," said Alice,
"that it was our favorite kind."
"Yes," Alvin said. "Chocolate marshmallow!"

Look Who's Part of the Children's Choice® Family!

Something special for Children's Choice® Book Club members

You can get all these storybook favorites—Puss in Boots, Babar, Curious George, Lyle, George and Martha and The Year at Maple Hill Farm—to hang up on your wall. They're big (17″ × 22″) and beautiful posters, printed in full color on high quality paper. Best of all, you can get all 6 for just $3.95, including postage and handling.

Please allow 3-6 weeks for delivery. Your posters are mailed in a tube, so they won't be creased at all.

Offer expires August 31, 1981

To order your set of 6 Children's Choice® posters, please send your name, address and $3.95 in check or money order to:

**CHILDREN'S CHOICE®
POSTERS
2931 East McCarty St.
P.O. Box 1068
Jefferson City, Mo. 65102**